Colourea
Socks

A ZEBRA BOOK
Written by David Lloyd
Illustrated by Malcolm Livingstone

PUBLISHED BY
WALKER BOOKS
LONDON

Ben was getting dressed.
Polly was helping.
There was only one sock.

Polly hunted through
the sock drawer.
Socks flew everywhere.
'Find the other red one,'
she said to Ben.

Ben toddled among
the socks.
He was looking at
the colours.

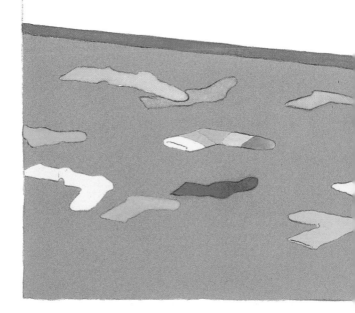

He picked up a green sock
and started to suck it.

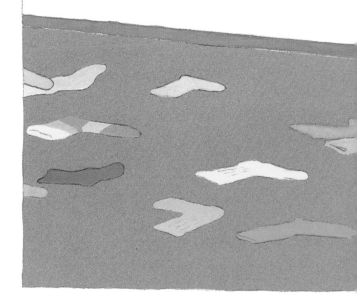

'Find a red sock like
the other one,' Polly said.

Ben dropped the green one
and picked up a yellow one.

Ben tried to put the
yellow sock on top of the
red sock.
'Oh no, Ben,' Polly said.

'Here's the other red one,' Polly said.

Ben took off the yellow
sock with the first red
sock inside it.
He pushed them up
his jumper.

Polly played a tickling
game with Ben's toes.

'We'll put the socks in
pairs,' Polly said.
She started sorting out
the colours.

Ben sucked his big
toe and watched.

Ben decided to help.
He mixed up all
the colours.
Polly got angry.

Polly picked up the
blue socks.
'Sit still, Ben,' she said.
Ben wriggled and kicked.
He didn't want to wear
blue socks.

'Which ones, then?'
Polly asked.
'Red? Yellow? Green?'
Ben wrinkled up his nose.
He knew which pair
he wanted.

The stripey pair, of course.
The socks with all the colours.
'Benbo buns,' Ben called them.
'Rainbow ones,
you mean,' said Polly.